KU-654-845

PUFFIN BOOKS

BAD BECKY

Gervase Phinn is a teacher, freelance lecturer, author, poet, educational consultant, school inspector, visiting professor of education and last, but by no means least, father of four. Most of his time is spent in schools with teachers and children. Gervase lives in Doncaster with his family.

GERVASE PHINN

Bad Becky

Illustrated by Lindsey Gardiner

PUFFIN

For Christine, the best sister a brother could have

PUFFIN BOOKS

Published by the Penguin Group
Penguin Books Ltd, 80 Strand, London WC2R 0RL, England
Penguin Group (USA), Inc., 375 Hudson Street, New York, New York 10014, USA
Penguin Books Australia Ltd, 250 Camberwell Road, Camberwell, Victoria 3124, Australia
Penguin Books Canada Ltd, 10 Alcorn Avenue, Toronto, Ontario, Canada M4V 3B2
Penguin Books India (P) Ltd, 11 Community Centre, Panchsheel Park, New Delhi – 110 017, India
Penguin Group (NZ), cnr Airborne and Rosedale Roads, Albany, Auckland 1310, New Zealand
Penguin Books (South Africa) (Pty) Ltd, 24 Sturdee Avenue, Rosebank 2196, South Africa

Penguin Books Ltd, Registered Offices: 80 Strand, London WC2R 0RL, England

www.penguin.com

First published 2004

3

Text copyright © Gervase Phinn, 2004
Illustrations copyright © Lindsey Gardiner, 2004
All rights reserved

The moral right of the author and illustrator has been asserted

Set in Perpetua

Made and printed in England by Clays Ltd, St Ives plc

Except in the United States of America, this book is sold subject to the condition that it shall not, by way of trade or
otherwise, be lent, re-sold, hired out, or otherwise circulated without the publisher's prior consent in any form of
binding or cover other than that in which it is published and without a similar condition including this condition being
imposed on the subsequent purchaser

British Library Cataloguing in Publication Data
A CIP catalogue record for this book is available from the British Library

ISBN 0–141–31807–4

Contents

Becky Hears a Story

Miss Drear opened the big coloured picture book and smiled widely. 'Today, children, I'm going to read a lovely story about a beautiful princess,' she said sweetly.

Oh no, thought Becky, not one of those boring old stories about

silly princesses and daring knights
in shining armour, where the poor
dragon is killed and everything
ends happily ever after.

Why couldn't her teacher read an
exciting story about blood-sucking
monsters, or nasty green aliens, or
headless ghosts? 'Oh phooey!' she cried
loudly. 'I hate beautiful princesses.'

'No, you
don't, Becky,'
said Miss Drear,
her smile
getting wider.

'Yes I do too,' said Becky, pulling her
most awful face to wind up the teacher.

'I like beautiful princesses,' trilled Araminta. 'I think they are nice.'

Well, of course Araminta *would* love a story about a princess, thought Becky. She came to school dressed like someone out of a fairy story – with her long golden curls tied in red silk ribbons, her little velvet dress with pearl buttons and lace collar, her white frilly socks that never seemed to get dirty and her shiny black shoes with tiny pink bows on the front. Araminta was never naughty; she was nice

and tidy and always polite and well
mannered. Which is exactly why she
really annoyed Becky, who was quite the
opposite.

Becky was the
youngest in her
family. She had
older twin brothers,
Bernard and Ben,
and she much
preferred playing
soldiers with
them, climbing trees, balancing on
walls, fishing in the canal, having
water fights, making mud pies and
kicking a football, to sitting in her

room with a doll on her knee.

'I've got a Sleeping Beauty doll,' Araminta continued, 'and I'm getting Prince Charming for Christmas.'

'Well, I don't like princesses,' mumbled Becky. 'They're soppy.'

'I'm sure every little girl dreams of growing up into a beautiful princess,' said Miss Drear, still smiling and peering over the top of her big round glasses. 'I know I did when I was a little girl.'

Becky thought that Miss Drear looked like the grinning green frog with the yellow eyes that lived in the school pond. She did not look at all like a beautiful princess.

'I'd like to grow up into a beautiful princess,' said Araminta.

'When I grow up,' said Becky, 'I want to be an astronaut, or a fighter pilot, or a deep-sea diver, or a boxer, or a soldier, not a soppy old princess.'

'That will do, Rebecca!' snapped Miss Drear. The teacher only called Becky Rebecca when she was cross with her and it was clear she was cross with her now. 'With all this chatter, we'll never get to my story about the beautiful princess.'

'Goody,' said Becky. 'Can we have a story about killer aliens from space instead?'

'And any more from you, Rebecca,' said Miss Drear, giving Becky her best rattlesnake look, 'and you will stand all by yourself in the corridor.' She turned the first page of the book, coughed lightly and read, '"Once upon a time, long long ago, there lived a beautiful princess. She had long golden hair, big blue eyes and soft skin, and her lips were as red as –"'

'Blood!' shouted out Becky.

'No, not blood,' said Miss Drear. '"She had lips as red as shiny cherries."'

'I hate cherries,' said Becky. 'They have stones. I once got a stone stuck in my throat and I nearly choked.'

'I like cherries,' said Araminta. 'I think they are nice.'

Miss Drear stared at Becky for a moment and then continued. '"And the beautiful princess was called –"'

'Doris,' said Becky.

'No, not Doris,' said the teacher.

'Why can't she be called Doris?' asked Becky.

'Because beautiful princesses are not called Doris, that's why,' said Miss Drear sharply.

'My granny's called Doris,' Becky told everyone.

'Well, this princess was not called Doris,' said the teacher firmly. 'She was called Princess Charisma and she lived –'

'In a dark, smelly, stinky old cobwebby castle full of spooks and skeletons and dead bodies,' said Becky, grinning ghoulishly at the rest of the class.

'No, she did not,' said Miss Drear, trying to keep her temper. 'She lived in a tall grey castle with steep walls, hidden away in the middle of an enchanted forest.' Then, more calmly, the teacher read on, '"One day, Princess Charisma was looking out of a window high up in the castle wall, when –"'

'She fell out!' cried Becky.

'No, she did *not* fall out!' said Miss Drear crossly. 'And if you don't listen and stop interrupting, Rebecca, *you* and *I* will fall out.'

'Well, I think this story's boring,' said Becky. 'Can't we have a story about a blood-sucking monster?'

'No, we cannot!' snapped the teacher.

'I don't like monsters,' said Araminta. 'I think they are scary.'

'That's because you're soppy,' sneered Becky.

'"Suddenly",' continued the teacher, '"the beautiful Princess Charisma saw a thick cloud of dust in the distance —"'

'It was a nasty dragon,' squealed Becky, 'with sharp teeth and blood-red eyes and long claws and fire coming out of its mouth. And it

had come to eat up Princess Charisma!'

'It was not a dragon,' said Miss Drear, through gritted teeth. 'It was a handsome prince.'

'I hate handsome princes,' moaned Becky, pulling another horrid face.

'I would like to be a handsome prince when I grow up,' said Simon.

'And I'd like to marry a handsome prince,' sighed Araminta in a syrupy voice.

'Well, I'd like to marry Cut-Throat Jake, the pirate,' said Becky, 'with his bushy beard and big black patch over his eye, and his great big silver hook and shiny cutlass, and his two big pistols and his squawking parrot that says rude words.'

'If you don't listen, Rebecca,' retorted Miss Drear, fast losing her patience, 'you will stand in the corridor all by yourself. Now, "Along the road came a handsome prince on his big white horse. Clip clop, clip clop, he went, across the little wooden bridge until –"'

'He fell off the bridge and into the river!' shouted Becky. 'And he floated downstream and there were crocodiles and alligators in the water with massive jaws and sharp teeth and they went snip snap, snip snap, chomp, chomp, chomp, chomp and they gobbled up the prince.'

Miss Drear had stopped smiling long ago. She was now beginning to look like Mr Scowler's dog when it growled and curled its lip. Mr Scowler was the school caretaker who never smiled and always said Becky was the most disobedient and difficult child he had ever met. Becky didn't like Mr Scowler either.

'Go and stand in the corridor, please, Rebecca,' ordered Miss Drear. 'I warned you not to keep on interrupting. You will stay there until you can behave yourself and learn not to shout out in class.'

Becky liked it in the corridor. It was far more interesting than listening to

some stupid story about boring Princess
Charisma and the wimpy prince. She
knew what would happen anyway. Fairy
stories always ended up with the prince
rescuing the princess and the two of
them riding off through the enchanted
forest and across the little wooden
bridge and living happily ever after.
Soppy! Soppy! Soppy! she thought.

On the Nature Table in the corridor
was a large glass tank. On the front was
a label that read MINIBEASTS. It was
full of caterpillars and maggots and
spiders and ants and earwigs and
crane flies and beetles and other
glorious creepy-crawlies. Becky loved

creepy-crawlies and often went
searching for them in the garden at
home, or in the dark corners of
the house. She collected them in
matchboxes and jam jars, and
sometimes, when her brothers teased
her, she put them in their beds. How
they shrieked when they found a fat
black spider with long hairy legs

scuttling across their pillows, or a long brown earwig wriggling over their sheets. They weren't such big boys then!

DO NOT TOUCH was written in bold black letters on the front of the tank.

'Huh!' said Becky, lifting the lid. 'We'll see about that!'

She reached inside and took out all the creepy-crawlies, one by one, and put them on the table. They wriggled and wiggled, squirmed and scuttled, slithered and crawled. This was fun, thought Becky, cradling a huge shiny black beetle in her hand. It tickled. Then she heard the unmistakeable footsteps of grumpy Mrs Groucher, the head teacher. Becky quickly stuffed all the creepy-crawlies into her pockets, scooping up the last earwig just as Mrs Groucher appeared round the corner.

'And what are you doing out of the classroom, Rebecca?' boomed the head marching towards her with a stern expression on her round red face. She had a voice like a foghorn and looked like a hippopotamus.

'Well, Rebecca?' grunted Mrs Groucher. 'Why are you standing in the corridor?'

'I've been sent out, Mrs Groucher,' Becky told her sweetly.

'Sent out!' repeated the head teacher. 'You are not in trouble again, are you?'

'Oh no, Mrs Groucher,' said Becky, putting on her most innocent voice. 'It's just that Miss Drear is reading a really scary story about man-eating monsters and killer aliens from outer space, and it  frightened me so much that she said I could stay out in the corridor until she has finished.' Then she added, 'I like stories about beautiful princesses and handsome princes.'

'Mmmm,' hummed the head teacher. 'Monsters, eh? Aliens from outer space?' She peered through the classroom window. 'Well, it looks as if the story is over now. You may return to your class.'

'Yes, Mrs Groucher,' said Becky, as if butter wouldn't melt in her mouth. 'Thank you so much, Mrs Groucher.'

'I thought I told you to wait in the corridor, Rebecca,' said Miss Drear when Becky appeared at the door.

'Mrs Groucher told me I had to

return to the classroom,' Becky replied triumphantly.

'Well, sit down and be quiet,' said Miss Drear. 'We are all writing stories about Princess Charisma and the handsome prince.'

'Can I write about a monster?' asked Becky.

'No!' snapped the teacher.

'An alien from outer space?'

'Certainly not!'

'But I didn't hear the story about Princess Charisma and the handsome prince,' whined Becky.

'Well, make it up,' Miss Drear told her.

'I've nearly finished mine,' said Araminta smugly.

'I bet it's soppy,' said Becky, under her breath.

'I've got to the part where Princess Charisma marries the handsome prince,' said Simon.

'Huh, well *there's* a surprise,' said Becky, and then she started writing. Her story was about a slimy green monster with sharp teeth and long claws that climbed up the castle wall and swallowed the beautiful Princess Charisma in one great gulp. Then it chased the handsome prince across the little wooden bridge and gobbled him up.

Becky was so busy writing she didn't notice that all the caterpillars and maggots and spiders and ants and earwigs and crane flies and beetles and other glorious creepy-crawlies were escaping from her pocket. They wriggled and wiggled, squirmed and scuttled, slithered and crawled across the desks.

'Aaaaaaahhhhhhhheeeeeeeooooo!'
screamed Araminta. 'There's a spider on
my hand, and an earwig on my leg, and
a maggot on my shoulder and a
caterpillar on my head!' Then she began

shouting and shrieking and running round and round the classroom like a cat with its tail on fire. Soon all the children were doing the same. All, that is, except Becky, who was so involved in her incredibly gruesome story that she did not notice the commotion going on around her.

Mrs Groucher thundered through the door. 'Sit down at once, children!' she roared. 'Whatever is this terrible noise?'

Miss Drear was standing trembling on a chair surrounded by minibeasts. She hated creepy-crawlies. Becky was sitting silently and putting the finishing touches to her story.

'I'm glad to see that at least one child in this class is being sensible,' said the head teacher, noticing Becky. 'And getting on quietly with her work.'

'Thank you, Mrs Groucher,' said Becky, smiling widely like the green frog with the biggest grin in the school pond.

Becky and the Visitor

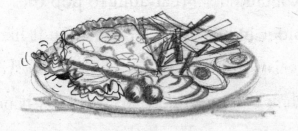

'Now I want you to be on your very best behaviour today, Becky,' said Mum. 'You know what happened last time Great-Aunt Mildred came to visit.'

Becky remembered what happened last time Great-Aunt Mildred came to visit very well indeed. At teatime, she had put a plastic spider underneath the lettuce on Great-Aunt Mildred's plate. It had only been a joke and she hadn't expected her great-aunt to pop the spider in her mouth, crunch on it like a crisp and then scream her head off when she took it out to see what it was. It was only a little spider.

And it was obviously made of plastic. Some people have no sense of humour, Becky had thought to herself when she had been sent to her room.

Great-Aunt Mildred was awful. She was always telling Becky what to do: 'Sit up properly!' 'Don't slouch!' 'Wipe your nose!' 'Take your elbows off the table!' 'Don't speak with your mouth full!' 'Use a tissue!' 'Don't cross your legs!' 'Speak nicely!' Nag nag nag nag nag. And then Great-Aunt Mildred would tell Becky what a good little girl *she* used to be when *she* was Becky's age, how *she* came top in everything at school and was best at sports and music and art and everything else you might care to mention. Huh, thought Becky, I bet she was a real teacher's pet and I would never *ever* want to be like her.

Now Great-Aunt Mildred was coming to visit again and so Becky had to be on her very best behaviour. She could not think of a more boring way of spending a Sunday afternoon than sitting in front of Great-Aunt Mildred, listening to her rambling on and on like a boring television programme that you couldn't turn off, and then having to watch her chomp her way through all the food put in front of her like some kind of starving dinosaur. Becky longed to be out in the sunshine, chasing her brothers or climbing trees.

'Are you going to put on that nice new dress with the white lace collar and your shiny black shoes?' Mum asked Becky. 'And you look lovely with pink ribbons in your hair.'

No way, thought Becky. The last person in the world she wanted to look like was Araminta. 'I like my T-shirt and jeans and my trainers,' she said stubbornly.

Becky rarely wore anything else when she was at home. She hated dresses and ribbons and white socks and shiny black party shoes. Pink was her worst colour – Becky liked navy and other less girly colours.

However, she knew making Mum cross wouldn't help to get her own way, so she decided to try her cute look. She gazed up at Mum with her huge green eyes and a shy smile broke across her freckly face as she slowly hooked a finger into her tangle of red curls.

'Your brothers look really smart in their new suits,' Dad piped up, folding away his newspaper. 'Wouldn't you like to look really smart in your nice new dress?'

'No thank you,' said Becky politely. 'I like my T-shirt and jeans.'

'You would look really pretty,' wheedled Dad.

'I don't want to look really pretty,' Becky replied slowly, trying her hardest not to be rude.

'Oh very well,' said Mum, 'suit yourself.'

Yes! It had worked.

'Bing-bong! Bing-bong! Bing-bong!'

went the doorbell.

'That will be Great-Aunt Mildred,' said Mum. Becky noticed that she didn't sound very enthusiastic. 'Now remember what I said, Becky.'

'Uuuugh,' grunted Becky in reply, dropping the angelic act.

In the hall, Dad, Mum and the brothers greeted Great-Aunt Mildred as she struggled to get through the door. Becky stood at the back, watching. Great-Aunt Mildred was a very big woman and she was wearing a hideous pink dress shaped like a tent and a huge floppy hat covered in flowers. She carried a massive bag over one arm and had a little dog tucked under the other. Becky had never seen such an ugly dog. It looked as if it had walked into a door and squashed its face. It had

enormous staring eyes, a fat round body and a stumpy tail, and its constant growling sounded like the rumble of a distant train. It was horrible.

'Hello, everyone!' boomed Great-Aunt Mildred. 'Say hello, Poochie.'

The dog growled a bit more loudly
and showed a set of sharp pointed teeth.

'Hello, Aunt Mildred,' said Dad
cheerfully.

'Hello, Aunt Mildred,' echoed Mum
with slightly less enthusiasm.

'Hello, Great-Aunt Mildred,' said the
brothers in unison.

'I've had a terrible journey,' said
Great-Aunt Mildred, puffing and panting
and marching into the front room.

Here we go, thought Becky. Hardly
through the door and she starts
complaining as usual.

'The traffic is terrible these days,'
grumbled Great-Aunt Mildred,
lowering herself into a chair. 'Mad
drivers, children on bikes, lorries
belching out fumes, buses crawling
along. My poor little Poochie is all hot
and thirsty, aren't you, Poochie?'

The dog growled even more loudly
and Great-Aunt Mildred thrust him into
Dad's hands. 'Fetch Poochie a bowl of

water,' she commanded. 'And make sure it's cold.'

'Yes, Aunt Mildred,' said Dad, disappearing into the kitchen with the dog and a none-too-pleased expression on his face.

'My, my, my,' said Great-Aunt Mildred, looking at the twins approvingly, 'what big boys you are now. Come and give your Great-Aunt Mildred a kiss.'

'Yuck!' shuddered Becky. Even the thought of those big wet slobbery kisses made her feel sick.

'Slurp, slurp, slurp,' went Great-Aunt Mildred, kissing the boys and covering their cheeks with bright red lipstick.

Becky thought that Ben and Bernard
looked as if they were being devoured
by an enormous pink jellyfish. There is
no way, thought Becky, that she was
going to let Great-Aunt Mildred slobber
over her like that.

'Hello, Rebecca,' said Great-Aunt
Mildred, screwing up her face as if she
were sucking a
lemon. 'I hope
you have learnt
to behave
yourself.'
'Oh yes, Great-
Aunt Mildred,' said Becky sweetly.

'Well, come and give your Great-
Aunt Mildred a big, big kiss.'

'I'd love to,' lied Becky, 'but I've just
got over chickenpox. My face was
covered in red spots the size of
mountains and I was scratching and
scratching all day long.'

Mum glared at Becky. She had *never* had chickenpox.

'Oh dear,' said Great-Aunt Mildred. 'I don't think you ought to come too close to me then.'

'Neither do I, Great-Aunt Mildred. I would hate you to catch it,' Becky replied, thinking she'd actually like nothing better.

'Whatever are you wearing, child?' asked Great-Aunt Mildred next.

'My jeans and T-shirt,' said Becky cheerfully.

'Little girls should wear nice colourful dresses and ribbons in their hair and dainty shoes,' said Great-Aunt

Mildred, 'and not jeans and T-shirts. When *I* was a little girl everyone said how pretty I looked in my party dress. I was the prettiest girl in school.'

At that moment there was a terrible scream from the kitchen. The noise was something like 'Oooeeeaaarrrggghhh!' and was followed by Dad rushing

 through the door. 'I've been bitten!' he cried, waving a very red-looking finger in the air and pulling

an excruciating face. 'I've been bitten!
The dog bit me!'

'You probably frightened him,'
said Great-Aunt Mildred, quite
unconcerned about Dad's suffering.
'Where is my little Poochie?' The dog
trotted towards her and jumped up on
to her lap. 'Did that big, big man
fwighten you, Poochie?' she asked the
dog in a silly voice that made Becky
cringe.

Dad glowered before going in search
of a plaster.

'Why don't you boys take Poochie
into the garden?' said Great-Aunt
Mildred. 'He's been in a hot stuffy car

all morning.' She tickled the dog under his chubby little chin. 'Does my ickle Poochie-Woochie want walkie-walkies?' she asked. 'Does he? Yes, he does.'

Bernard and Ben reluctantly and very carefully attached the fat unfriendly creature to his lead and led him out towards the back garden.

He growled at the brothers, baring his sharp teeth and sticking his stumpy little tail bolt upright. Becky could see that her brothers were not at all keen on taking the savage little brute for 'walkie-walkies', but she knew that they had no choice.

'Would you like a cup of tea, Aunt Mildred,' asked Mum, 'and a piece of chocolate cake that I've baked specially?'

'Yes, I would,' said Great-Aunt Mildred – without saying please, Becky noticed. 'I love chocolate cake. I bake delicious chocolate cakes myself. Everyone says they are as light as a feather.'

45

At that moment there was a terrible shriek from the garden. The noise sounded like 'Eeeaaarrroooggghhh!' and, seconds later, Bernard and Ben rushed through the door with the dog snapping at their heels.

'Get it off!' cried Ben, hiding behind the table.

'Get it off!' echoed Bernard, climbing on a chair.

'It's ripped my new coat!' wailed Ben.

'And torn my trousers!' moaned Bernard.

'He must be hungry,' said Great-Aunt Mildred. 'Does my ickle Poochie-

Woochie want his din-dins?' she asked.
'Does he? Yes, he does.' She dug into her
large bag and took out an enormous
packet of dog biscuits and a huge tin of
dog food. She thrust them towards
Becky. 'Get him his dinner,' she said,
'and don't give too much.'

'Do I have to?' Becky asked, scowling
as she reluctantly took the dog food.

'Yes, you do,' replied Great-Aunt
Mildred. 'Good little girls do as they are
told, and they are seen but not heard.'

Becky looked down at the dog. He
looked back at her with the unblinking
stare of a killer shark. 'Come on then,'
she said.

Poochie obediently trotted into the kitchen behind Becky. But as soon as she started shaking some biscuits into a bowl, the dog edged towards her, growling, his sharp teeth gleaming.

Becky stopped what she was doing, put her hands on her hips and stared into Poochie's eyes. It was her really, really angry stare. Mum said it was a stare that could turn milk sour and freeze soup in pans. Then she stabbed the air with a finger. 'Be quiet! You silly dog!' she shouted. 'One more growl out of you and I'll lock you in the store cupboard where it's dark and spooky.'

Poochie gazed at her for a moment

and the growl died in his throat. Then
he whimpered and stuck his tail
between his legs as he scuttled into a
corner.

'Now sit,' ordered Becky, 'and behave yourself!'

The dog did as he was told; he had met his match.

When Becky went back to the living room Great-Aunt Mildred was devouring a large piece of chocolate cake. She looked like a monster chomping away, thought Becky. Chomp, chomp, chomp.

'It's not as nice as the chocolate cake I make,' Great-Aunt Mildred was telling Mum. 'Mine is much lighter and has more chocolate in it. I have won prizes with my chocolate cake.'

Becky sniffed. Huh, she thought, I bet she has.

'Blow your nose, Becky,' said Great-Aunt Mildred. 'Nice little girls don't sniff and snuffle like anteaters.'

Becky wished there were such things as Aunt Eaters. Great lumbering, red-eyed, dribbling monsters with gnashing teeth and great slashing claws that went in search of horrible aunts and gobbled them up. Aunt Mildred took another huge mouthful of chocolate cake.

Becky dug deep into the pockets of

her jeans for a handkerchief – and then she felt them. The maggots! She had forgotten about the maggots. She had put them in there when she and the brothers had gone fishing the day before.

'What have you got in your pocket?' asked Great-Aunt Mildred, munching away on the chocolate cake.

'Nothing, Great-Aunt Mildred,' replied Becky.

'Yes, you have. You're fiddling with something.'

'No, I'm not,' said Becky, wishing she would mind her own business for once.

'Yes, you are,' Great-Aunt Mildred

persisted, spitting out bits of chocolate cake as she talked.

Becky felt like telling her that it is very bad manners to speak with your mouth full, but she merely said, 'It's nothing really.'

'Let me see, child,' said Aunt Mildred, holding out her hand.

'I'd rather not,' said Becky.

'I insist,' said Great-Aunt Mildred angrily. 'Do as you are told.'

'Very well,' said Becky, and she scooped out a handful of wriggling maggots and placed them in Great-Aunt Mildred's hand.

'AAAAhhhhhhuuuuuggggg!'

screamed Great-Aunt Mildred. Her hand shot up and all the maggots flew into the air. Becky couldn't believe her eyes as she watched one or two of them land neatly down the front of her great-aunt's dress.

Letting her plate of chocolate cake slide to the floor, Great-Aunt Mildred leapt to her feet and shot out of the door like a stampeding elephant, followed by a yelping Poochie.

After the front door had slammed behind her, Mum, Dad, the brothers and Becky shuffled into the kitchen, each one of them lost for words. They sat down at the kitchen table, all a bit

dishevelled and badly in need of a cup
of tea.

'She said my chocolate cake wasn't
very nice,' said Mum glumly as she
poured the tea.

'My finger hurts,' said Dad angrily. 'Nasty dog!'

'My new jacket is ruined!' grumbled Ben.

'So are my new trousers!' complained Bernard.

Becky stayed completely silent. She was waiting for her telling-off to start.

Then something totally unexpected happened.

'I suppose we'll not be seeing Great-Aunt Mildred for quite some time,' said Mum, the corners of her mouth twitching. Becky couldn't believe it – her mum wasn't cross at all – she was trying to stop herself from smiling!

'I think you're right,' replied Dad, with an unmistakable grin on his face.

Becky looked at her mum and dad, and then at the brothers, who were smirking like mad.

They all looked at Becky. Then Dad slid a plate across the table. On it was the last slice of chocolate cake.

Becky's mouth began to water. It was a huge wedge of dark mouth-watering sponge with sweet creamy filling and a thick crust of icing on the top. Her absolute favourite.

'I think Becky deserves this,' Dad said, and the rest of the family nodded in agreement.

Perhaps having Great-Aunt Mildred to tea wasn't all bad, Becky thought to herself as she took her first enormous bite of chocolate cake.

The Birthday Party

'I don't want to go to Simon's birthday party!' cried Becky, stamping her foot and pushing out her bottom lip.

Becky knew this little outburst was a bit babyish but it was one of her favourite means of getting her own way. If Mum didn't feel up to an argument, she would usually sigh and shake her head and give in with the words, 'Oh very well, suit yourself.'

That morning, however, the tactic was not working. Mum was not in the mood to be disobeyed.

'Well, you're going,' said Mum firmly. 'You're lucky to get an invitation. And no more arguing, young lady, or you'll go to your room for the rest of the day.'

'But –' began Becky, thinking she would have another try.

'And no "buts",' interrupted Mum.

Wow, thought Becky. Mum sounded just like Mrs Groucher this morning.

Becky put on her best sulky face. 'It'll be really soppy, I know it will,' she said. 'All the boys will be kicking a football or climbing trees and they won't let me join in, and all the girls will be playing with dolls or dressing up, and I *definitely* don't want to join in with that.'

'And, of course, there'll be horrible raspberry jelly and ice cream and nasty buns and awful chocolate cake,' said Dad with a grin.

'And a party bag for everyone,' said

Ben. 'You won't want that.'

'And there'll be a magician,' said Bernard. 'He'll be very boring.'

For one reason or another, each member of the family was very keen that Becky should be out of the way that Saturday afternoon. Mum wanted to go Christmas shopping in town, and buying presents for the children would be impossible with her sharp-eyed daughter watching her every move. Dad was hoping to have a quiet time watching the football on the television, and the brothers had two friends coming round and they didn't want their little sister spoiling things. They all looked at Becky hopefully.

Mmmm, she thought. All that yummy food and a party bag full of goodies and a magician as well. Perhaps it didn't sound that bad, after all. Becky imagined a table piled with all her favourite food. Then she imagined a tall wizard with a long white beard and flowing hair and fingers like twigs. He'd be dressed in a pointed hat, with a cloak glittering with stars and moons,

and he'd be holding a golden wand
ready to perform all sorts of magic.

'I'll go,' said Becky. 'But I'm not
wearing a stupid dress.'

All the children were gathered round
Simon giving him presents when Becky
arrived. Simon was a tall, pale-faced
boy with long lank hair and doleful
eyes. He wore large round glasses and
that afternoon was dressed in a red
waistcoat and matching bow tie.

'I've brought you a colouring book,'
chirruped Araminta to Simon. She
was wearing a bright pink dress
with a green sash and her hair was

in ringlets. 'It's got lots of lovely
pictures of animals for you to colour in.'

'Thank you,' said Simon, stroking the
cover of the book gently. 'It's super.'

'I've brought you a reading book,'
said Gareth. He wore a very clean white
shirt and tie and polished shoes. 'It's
called *Nice Stories for Children* and has
eighty pages.'

'Thank you,' said Simon again,
placing it next to the colouring book.
'It's just what I wanted.'

'And I've brought you a jigsaw of a
beautiful garden,' said Jade, thrusting a
parcel wrapped in silver paper into
Simon's hand. She too was in her best

party dress. 'It's got five hundred and
ninety-nine pieces.'

'Brilliant!' said Simon.

'Well, I've brought you an
intergalactic, space-zapping water
pistol,' said Becky.

Simon's mother, who was making
delighted sounds at all the presents up
to this point, suddenly gasped and
snatched the parcel from Becky's hands.
'I don't allow guns,' she said.

'That's OK,' said Becky, snatching it
back. 'I'll have it then.'

While the rest of the children played
Pass the Parcel, Musical Chairs and
other party games that Becky thought

were soppy, she filled the big green intergalactic, space-zapping water pistol.

She squirted the windows, she squirted the chairs, she squirted the ceiling, she squirted the floor. When she squirted Simon and made him cry, his mother told Becky that if she squirted one more time, she would be taken home.

'When is the magician coming?' asked Becky, stuffing the big green intergalactic, space-zapping water pistol in the back pocket of her jeans.

'After tea,' said Simon's mum. 'And you have to be very, very good or he'll turn you into a frog.'

Sometimes grown-ups say the most stupid things, thought Becky.

At tea, Becky ate three packets of crisps, six sandwiches, five buns, four bowls of ice cream and jelly and two pieces of chocolate cake. Then she flopped on the floor feeling nice and full.

At that moment the magician

arrived. He was not what Becky expected at all. Instead of a tall wizard with a long white beard and flowing hair, and fingers like twigs, a pointed hat, a cloak glittering with stars and moons and a golden wand, the magician was a small plump man with a shiny bald head and a very large red nose. He was dressed in a baggy red and yellow checked suit and wore a big spotted bow tie. He carried a large sack with Marvo the Magician written in silver letters on the front.

'Hello, children!' he shouted cheerfully, waving his hand in the air like a floppy daffodil in the wind.

'I'm the incredible Marvo the Magician.'

'You don't look like a magician,' said
Becky. 'You look like a clown.'

'Oh no, I don't!' snapped Marvo.

'Oh yes, you do,' snapped back
Becky.

Marvo decided to ignore her. 'Now children, I would like you all to gather here in front of me on the carpet.' Becky placed herself at the very front. The magician eyed her suspiciously before rummaging in his large sack. He brought out a silver wand. 'I can do a magic trick, with my little silver stick.'

'I thought magicians called them wands,' said Becky.

'Well, I call it a stick,' said Marvo, glaring at her. 'I wonder if some nice, well-behaved and very polite little boy or girl would like to come and help Marvo the Magician with his first magic trick?'

Becky was at his side before anyone else had time to blink.

'I'll help you,' she said.

Marvo pulled a face. 'What about somebody else?' he asked, looking around the room.

Becky glared fiercely at the other children who were sitting wide-eyed on the floor in front of the magician. It had the desired effect. Nobody moved.

'Very well,' said Marvo to Becky, 'but remember, Marvo only likes good little girls.'

'Can I look at your wand?' asked Becky, ignoring him and picking up the silver stick.

Marvo snatched it from her. 'Put it down!' he snapped.

'Can you turn people into frogs?' she asked.

'Don't be silly, of course not,' he replied, looking hot and flustered.

'Simon's mum said that if I wasn't very, very good you would turn *me* into a frog.'

'I wish I could,' murmured the magician.

'It might be good fun being a frog,' said Becky. 'I bet a real magician could turn somebody into a frog.'

'Now you have to be very quiet, little girl, otherwise you won't be able to

help me with my magic trick,' said
Marvo through gritted teeth.

'What do I have to do?' asked Becky.
She was hoping that Marvo would do
the trick where he put somebody in a
box and cut them in half with a big
silver saw.

'I'll tell you in a moment, if you'll
listen!' Marvo took a small black box
out of the large sack. 'Now, children, I
have here my magic box,' he said.

Becky grabbed it from his hand,
looked inside and tipped it up.

'Put it down!' ordered Marvo angrily.

'I was seeing if it was empty,' said
Becky.

'Well, wait until I tell you,' said Marvo. 'Now I want you to look in the box and make sure there is nothing inside.' He placed it before Becky.

'I've already looked,' said Becky.

'Well, look again,' growled the magician. She lifted the lid and peered inside. 'Is it empty?' he asked.

'Yes.'

'Are you sure?' asked Marvo.

'Yes.'

'Very sure?'

'Yes,' Becky said again, beginning to

feel impatient with his silly questions.

'Completely sure?'

'How many more times do I have to
tell you?' said Becky. 'There's *nothing*
in it!'

Marvo took a deep breath and let it
out very loudly. He was trying to stay
calm. 'Everyone has to be very quiet
now.' He looked meaningfully at Becky.
'I am going to close the lid of my
magic box and say the magic words,
Abracadabra! Abracadoo!, so listen and
watch really carefully, children.' Waving
his silver stick over the box, Marvo
chanted, 'Abracadabra! Abracadoo!
What's in the box? I will show it to you.

Here,' he said to Becky, 'hold my silver
wand, little girl.'

'You said it was called a stick,' said
Becky, who didn't like being called
'little girl' one bit.

'Well, it's now a wand!' he snapped.
'Just hold it and be
quiet.' Marvo lifted the
lid of the box
and reached
inside. 'What
have we here?'
He gasped
dramatically as
he produced a small furry white
toy rabbit.

'Where did you come from, little rabbit?' asked Marvo, with an amazed expression on his face.

'From up your sleeve,' said Becky.

'No, it didn't,' barked the magician.

'I saw you take it out of your sleeve when you put your hands in the box,' said Becky.

'No, you did not,' growled Marvo again.

'Yes, I did,' said Becky, placing her hands on her hips. 'You're a big fibber.'

'Go and sit down,' said Marvo angrily, 'and behave yourself. Now I want someone else to help me with my next magic trick. Where is the birthday boy?'

Simon put up his hand. 'Would you like to help me?' Simon shook his head. He looked sheepishly at Becky. 'Oh, come along,' said Marvo.

'I'll help you,' shouted Becky, who had taken up her position at the very front of the circle of children.

'No, you won't,' said the magician quickly, before she could get to her feet. 'I've had enough help from you.'

'I'll help you, Marvo,' said Araminta sweetly, jumping up, brushing down her dress and shaking her perfect golden curls.

'Come along then, little girl,' said Marvo, cheering up. Araminta looked a well-behaved little girl, just the sort of child he liked.

Araminta stood next to the magician and smiled sweetly. 'I like rabbits,' she told Marvo. 'They're nice.'

'Are you going to cut her in half?' asked Becky.

'No, I am not,' replied Marvo. 'Why don't you go and sit at the back.'

'I like it here,' Becky said, shuffling forward.

'Now, for my next trick, I have Marvo's magic candles.' He placed three large coloured candles on the table behind him. 'I am going to ask this little girl to light them.'

'Children shouldn't play with matches,' said Becky. 'My dad says it's very dangerous.'

'I am watching her very carefully,' said Marvo.

'She might set fire to something.'

'She won't,' said Marvo. He smiled at the rest of the children. 'I am going to ask this little girl to light the candles and then, by magic, I am going to make them go out and then light themselves again.'

What a silly trick, thought Becky. Anybody could do that. On her birthday cake Mum had put these candles which relit themselves as if by magic. You could buy them from the shops.

'I am now going to make the candles go out for the first time,' continued Marvo in what Becky thought was a very childish voice.

'You could just blow them out,' said Becky, 'it would be easier.'

'When I wave my magic stick –'

'Wand,' corrected Becky.

'Stick!' said Marvo, glowering at her. 'When I wave my magic stick and say the magic words – and what are the magic words, children?'

'May I go to the toilet?' asked Becky.

'Don't interrupt!' exclaimed Marvo. 'When I say the magic words Abracadabra! Abracadoo –'

'I really would like to go to the loo,' said Becky.

'Off you go then,' said Marvo, quite relieved that the troublesome child would be out of his way.

Becky scurried off. She didn't really want to go to the toilet but was bored by Marvo and his silly tricks.

First she looked through Simon's presents. Nothing very interesting there, she thought. Lots of books and pens and socks and jumpers. Then she wandered into the kitchen and helped herself to a couple of sausage rolls, a sandwich, two buns and another slice of birthday cake.

When she returned a few minutes later the three coloured candles were burning brightly in front of the children.

'Thank you, little girl,' the magician was saying to Araminta. 'You can sit down again now.'

Becky watched as Marvo, waving his

magic stick above his head, chanted the magic words, 'Abracadabra! Abracadoo –'

She watched as Araminta skipped back to her place on the carpet, catching one of the candles with her elbow. The candle wobbled and then fell on to the other two candles with a clunk, knocking them to the floor.

This is more like it, thought Becky, as the candles instantly set light to some wrapping paper that had been left there.

Soon, red and yellow tongues of flame were licking up the tablecloth and causing it to flare and crackle as it burned.

'Aaaaaaahhh!' everyone screamed, jumping up and running as far away as possible. Simon's mother rushed into the room and immediately began screaming too.

But Becky didn't move. She was rooted to the spot, watching the chaos and panic around her in fascination. She didn't feel frightened at all. Dad had always said that in an emergency you should stay calm and decide on a clear plan of action. Marvo, she could see, was far from calm and clearly didn't know what to do. He jumped up and down frantically.

'Oh dear!' he panted, trying to beat out
the flames with his large sack. 'Fire!
Fire! Help! Help!'

This calls for action, thought Becky.

She pulled the big green intergalactic, space-zapping water pistol out of the back pocket of her jeans.

'Get back!' she shouted.

As the children ran about screaming and shouting and Marvo tried to stamp out the flames on his burning sack, Becky took aim and squirted.

Out of the barrel of the big green intergalactic, space-zapping water pistol came a long clear jet of water. Becky squirted and squirted and squirted until the fire was out.

All the children cheered, Simon's mum stared open-mouthed at the smouldering remains and Marvo the

magician stood in silence – completely
soaking wet and with a face like
thunder.

*

'This has been some party,' said Becky with real excitement in her voice, when everyone was ready to go home. 'The very best birthday party I have ever been to. It was fantastic!' She was clutching a particularly large goody bag.

'Oh, thank you, Becky dear,' said Simon's mother. 'If it hadn't been for you, the house would have burnt down.'

Becky watched Marvo – dripping and furious – creep out of the front door.

'It's a pity you didn't have a fire extinguisher up your sleeve,' shouted Becky as he made his way sheepishly down the garden path.